Owning up to LIES

Learning to tell the TRUTH

Jasmine Brooke

FOX EYE
PUBLISHING

Koala found it difficult to always tell the **TRUTH**. Sometimes, Koala **LIED**.

If Koala had done something **WRONG**, she found it hard to **OWN UP**. Sometimes, she just **KEPT QUIET**.

But not telling the **TRUTH** and not being **HONEST** could get Koala into **TROUBLE**.

Koala was excited. It was time for the class camping trip. "I am a great camper!" Koala boasted. But that wasn't quite the **TRUTH**.

When the class arrived at the campsite, Mrs Tree helped Rhino and Parrot with their tent. She helped Lion and Monkey too.

"I can pitch our tent!" Koala boasted to Crocodile. "I know exactly what to do." But Koala couldn't pitch a tent. She hadn't told the **TRUTH**.

That night, Lion and Monkey curled up in their tent. Rhino and Parrot were soon asleep. But when Crocodile and Koala climbed inside their tent, it crumpled in a heap.

"You can't pitch a tent!" spluttered Crocodile. "You told a silly **LIE**."

Mrs Tree helped Crocodile from the tent. She helped Koala too. "I think you'd better share my tent tonight," she told them both. "That's the most sensible thing to do."

Squashed in the tent, Koala began to wish that she had instead told the TRUTH.

In the morning, Koala shouted,
"I can fry eggs for breakfast!
I know exactly what to do."

But Koala burnt the eggs.
She didn't know what to do.

"You can't cook!" said Parrot. "That was another **LIE**."

Now everyone was hungry. Koala was too. As her tummy rumbled, she wished she had told the **TRUTH**.

11

In the afternoon, Mrs Tree said that they could all row the boat. "I'm a great rower," said Koala. But ... that's right – she really wasn't telling the **TRUTH!**

Before Mrs Tree could stop her, Koala grabbed the oars. But as she drifted away, Koala realised she really should have told the **TRUTH**.

"Hold on!" cried Mrs Tree, and she leant over with a branch. "Pull, everyone!" she called. "One, two, three!"

Everyone tugged and everyone heaved. They all pulled Koala in. Safely ashore once more, Koala sighed, "I'm sorry, everyone. I really can't row at all!"

"Well, Koala," smiled Mrs Tree. "You've **OWNED UP** and told the **TRUTH** - at last!"

The next day, it was time to go home. It was time to pack up the tents. "Do you know what to do?" Mrs Tree asked Koala.

TRUTHFULLY Koala said, "No, I haven't a clue!" Mrs Tree smiled and showed Koala exactly what to do.

Telling **LIES** had caused **TROUBLE**. It had almost spoilt the trip. Koala had learnt that being **HONEST** was exactly the best thing to do!

Words and feelings

Koala found it hard to tell the truth in this story. She found it hard to own up and that got her into a lot of trouble.

TRUTH

TROUBLE

There are a lot of words to do with being honest and telling the truth in this book. Can you remember all of them?

HONEST

LIE

OWNED UP

Let's talk about behaviour

This series helps children to understand and manage difficult emotions and behaviours. The animal characters in the series have been created to show human behaviour that is often seen in young children, and which they may find difficult to manage.

Owning Up to Lies

The story in this book examines issues around telling the truth. It looks at how telling lies and not owning up can affect people and those around them, too.

   The book is designed to show young children how they can manage their behaviour and learn to be truthful.

How to use this book

You can read this book with one child or a group of children. The book can be used to begin a discussion around complex behaviour such as telling the truth.

   The book is also a reading aid, with enlarged and repeated words to help children to develop their reading skills.

How to read the story

Before beginning the story, ensure that the children you are reading to are relaxed and focused.

Take time to look at the enlarged words and the illustrations, and discuss what this book might be about before reading the story.

New words can be tricky for young children to approach. Sounding them out first, slowly and repeatedly, can help children to learn the words and become familiar with them.

How to discuss the story

When you have finished reading the story, use these questions and discussion points to examine the theme of the story with children and explore the emotions and behaviours within it:

- What do you think the story was about? Have you been in a situation in which you didn't tell the truth? What was that situation? For example, did you tell a lie about something or didn't own up to something? Encourage the children to talk about their experiences.

- Talk about ways that people can cope with wanting to tell lies or not owning up. For example, think about the consequences of telling lies before doing so. Talk to the children about what tools they think might work for them and why.

- Discuss what it is like to cope with someone who tells lies. Explain that Koala told a lot of lies in the story, and that caused trouble both for her and those around her.

- Talk about why it is important to say sorry to someone you have upset. Discuss why this can make that person feel better, and the person who says sorry feel better, too.

Titles in the series

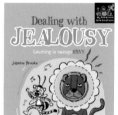

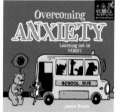

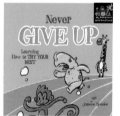

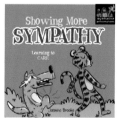

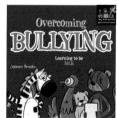

First published in 2023 by Fox Eye Publishing
Unit 31, Vulcan House Business Centre,
Vulcan Road, Leicester, LE5 3EF
www.foxeyepublishing.com

Author: Jasmine Brooke
Art director: Paul Phillips
Cover designer: Emma Bailey & Salma Thadha
Editor: Jenny Rush

All illustrations by Novel

ISBN 978-1-80445-296-7

A catalogue record for this book is available from the British
Library

Printed in China

David
and the
Hairy Beast

Fiona Veitch Smith

Illustrations by Amy Warmington

SPCK

First published in Great Britain in 2011 by Crafty Publishing
Newcastle-upon-Tyne

This edition published in Great Britain in 2015

Society for Promoting Christian Knowledge
36 Causton Street
London SW1P 4ST
www.spck.org.uk

British Library Cataloguing-in-Publication Data
A catalogue record for this book is available from the British Library

ISBN 978–0–281–07455–6

10 9 8 7 6 5 4 3 2 1

Printed in Great Britain by Micropress

Produced on paper from sustainable forests

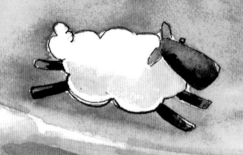

For Megan – FVS
For Joshua – AW

David... was the youngest of **seven brothers** and **two sisters,**

who lived together with their mum and dad on a
very busy farm near Bethlehem.

When each of the children
was big enough, their parents gave them
important jobs to do . . .

Eliab... was in charge of **taming**

wild stallions.

Abinidab &

Shannah

were in charge of feeding and **grooming**

a very angry bull.

were in charge of shearing the sheep . . .

and **selling the wool** to merchants at the market.

Nethanel

was in charge of keeping all the farm tools nice and **sharp.**

zeruiah & Abigail

were in charge of **baking bread**, making cakes and feeding their **hungry brothers.**

It was a big job because each boy would eat at least six loaves and three cakes **every single day.**

13

But David was in **charge of nothing.**

As far as he could tell, no one noticed him,
no one thought he was important

and **no one listened** to a thing he had to say.

So one day he decided to **tell his big brother** Eliab **how he** was feeling.

"It's not fair!" said David.

"Everyone's got a job to do, except me."

"But you're too little to work,"

said Eliab, from the back of a wild black horse.

"Why don't you just play with your toys like a good little boy
and leave the grown-up stuff to us?"

This made David very angry.

"**I'm not a little boy!** I'm nearly seven, and I'm **big** enough and **brave** enough to do anything you can do."

Eliab **just laughed** at this
and galloped away.

But David's dad had been listening
and he found his son sitting on the grass near the sheep pen.

"You know what, son?" he said. "I've got a very important job

:hat only the **bravest** of boys can do.

Some hairy beasts have been

attacking my sheep . . .

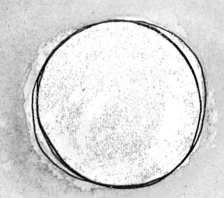

and I need someone to look after them.

Do you know anyone
who **can do the job?"**

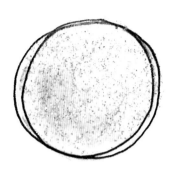

David wanted to jump up and down
and shout "ME! ME! ME!"
but there was **one thing** stopping him:
the **horrible hairy beasts.**

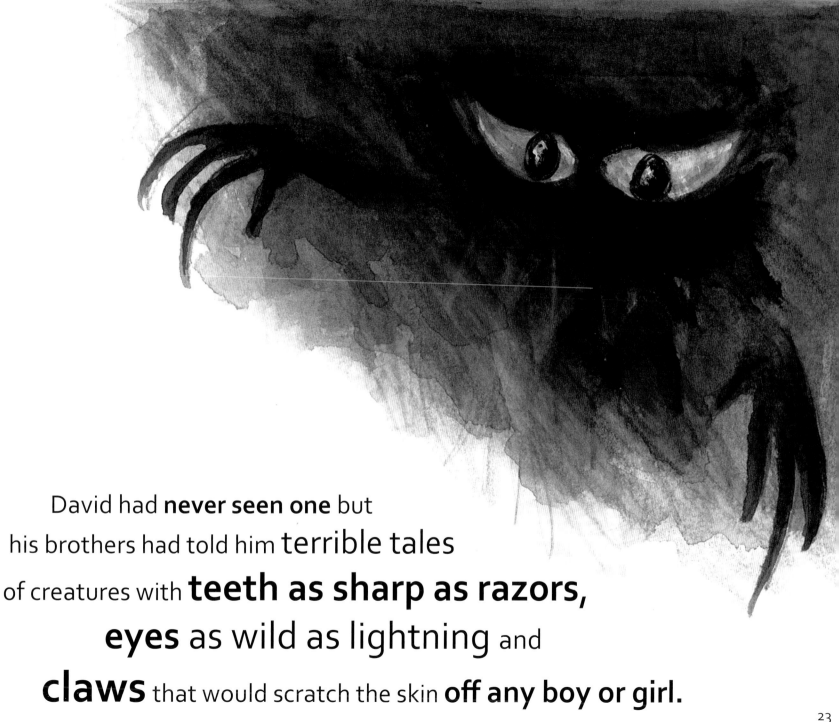

David had **never seen one** but
his brothers had told him terrible tales
of creatures with **teeth as sharp as razors,**
eyes as wild as lightning and
claws that would scratch the skin **off any boy or girl.**

23

David was **too scared to say "yes"** but too proud to say "no". He didn't know what to do, so he **decided to ask God.**

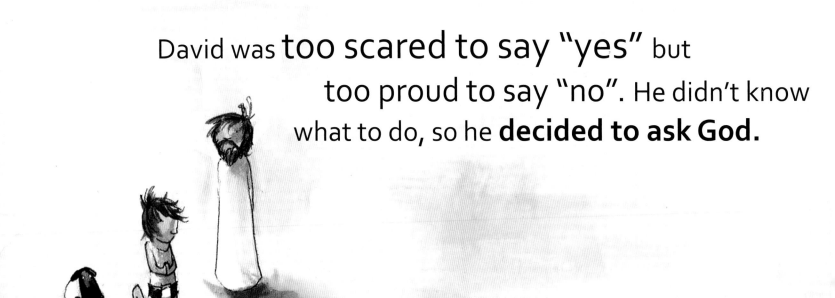

While his dad stood beside him, David closed his eyes, bowed his head and **said this prayer:**

"Dear God, please **give me the courage** to do this job and **protect me** from the hairy beasts. Amen." **Then David waited for an answer.**

He didn't have to wait long.

"You can do it!"

said a voice inside David's head

and, **as he heard it,**
he felt his heart beat as strong as a drum,
while **God filled him up with courage**. Then he opened his eyes,
took a deep breath and said to his dad:

"Yes, I can do it!"

That night, when his brothers and sisters had gone to bed, **David took his tent** and **camped out beside the sheep pen**.

David's dad had given him a catapult and a bag of stones and said:

"If a hairy beast comes out of the darkness, use this to scare it away."

So **David watched** the **shadows** to make sure **none of them moved.**

It was nearly dawn
before one of them did.

And its teeth were as **sharp as razors,**
its eyes as wild as **lightning**

and its claws were ready to scratch the skin off any
lamb that had become separated from its mother.

David grabbed his catapult,
fired a stone
and, with a yelp, the hairy beast scuttled back
into the darkness.

As the sun came up, David's whole family rushed out to see what had happened.
He stood there, smiling, with the catapult in his hand.

"See," he said to Eliab, "I'm jus

s brave as you."

"How did you do it?"
asked the eldest brother.

David's dad winked at him and said:
"With a little bit of courage and
a **lot of help from God.**"

David and the Hairy Beast is the first in the
Young David series.

Other books in the series:

David and the Kingmaker
ISBN 978 0 281 07456 3

David and the Giant
ISBN 978 0 281 07457 0

David and the Lonely Prince
ISBN 978 0 281 07458 7

David and the Grumpy King
ISBN 978 0 281 07459 4

***David and the
Never-ending Kingdom***
ISBN 978 0 281 07460 0

www.spck.org.uk
http://fiona.veitchsmith.com